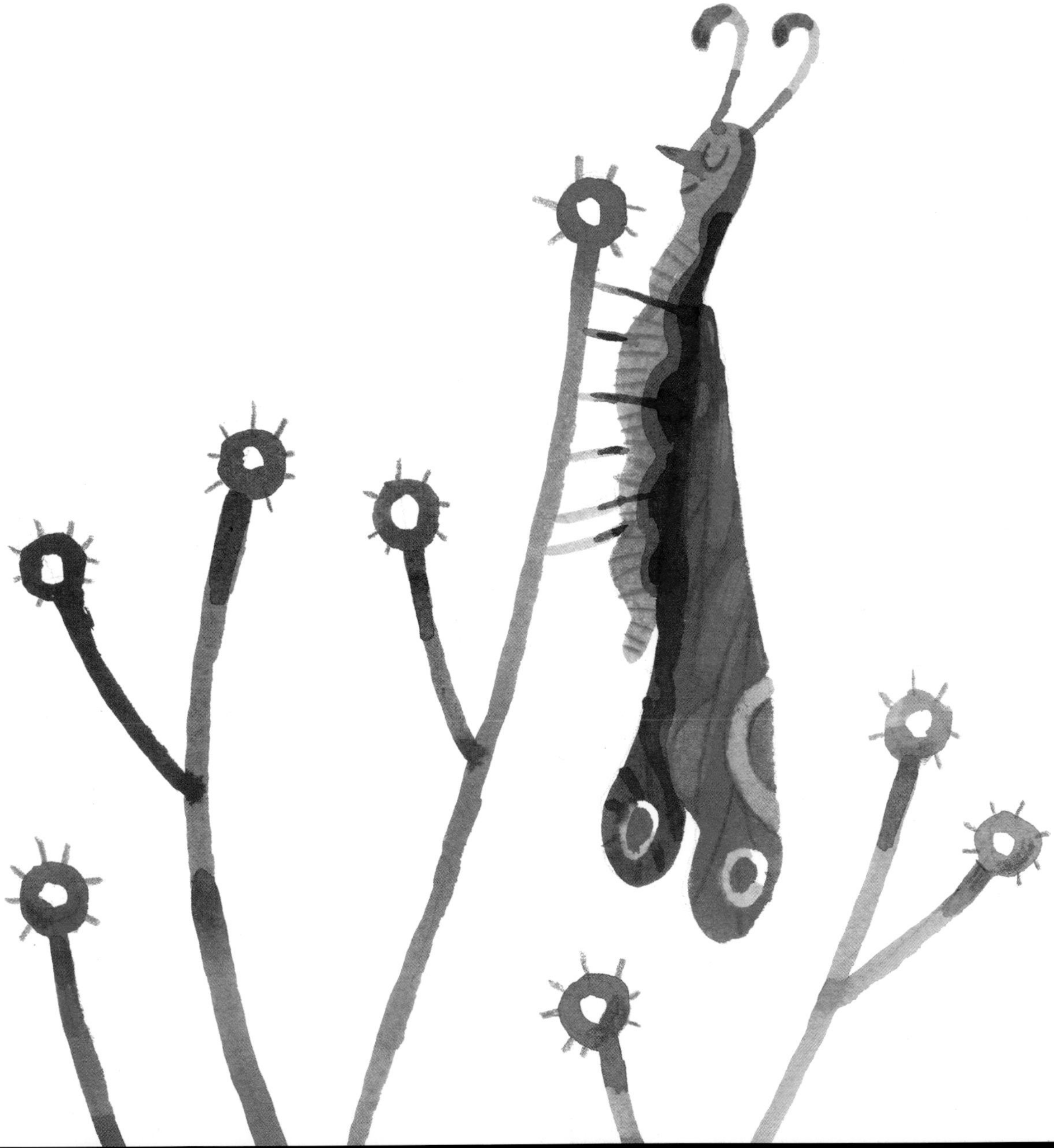

This one is for all of us — PS

For my father, Branislav, who showed me the beauty of the world — MP

Published in 2022 by Groundwood Books / House of Anansi Press
groundwoodbooks.com

Groundwood Books respectfully acknowledges that the land on which we operate is the Traditional Territory of many Nations, including the Anishinabeg, the Wendat and the Haudenosaunee. It is also the Treaty Lands of the Mississaugas of the Credit.

We gratefully acknowledge for their financial support of our publishing program the Canada Council for the Arts, the Ontario Arts Council and the Government of Canada.

Canada Council   Conseil des Arts
for the Arts   du Canada

ONTARIO ARTS COUNCIL
CONSEIL DES ARTS DE L'ONTARIO
an Ontario government agency
un organisme du gouvernement de l'Ontario

With the participation of the Government of Canada
Avec la participation du gouvernement du Canada | Canadä

Library and Archives Canada Cataloguing in Publication
Title: Sun wishes / by Patricia Storms ; pictures by Milan Pavlović.
Names: Storms, Patricia, author. | Pavlović, Milan (Illustrator), illustrator.
Identifiers: Canadiana (print) 20210236000 | Canadiana (ebook) 20210236019
| ISBN 9781773064505 (hardcover) | ISBN 9781773064512 (EPUB) |
ISBN 9781773064529 (Kindle)
Classification: LCC PS8637.T6755 S96 2022 | DDC jC813/.6—dc23

The illustrations were done in mixed media, drawing inks and color pencils.
Design by Michael Solomon
Printed and bound in South Korea

MIX
Paper from
responsible sources
FSC® C013572

SUN WISHES

by

PATRICIA STORMS

pictures by

MILAN PAVLOVIĆ

GROUNDWOOD BOOKS
HOUSE OF ANANSI PRESS
TORONTO / BERKELEY

If I were the sun, I would
sing a gentle morning song

to wake my slumbering friends.

I would bring jubilant color

into the gloomiest of days.

If I were the sun, I would inspire
a vivid tapestry,

and revel in the joys of
a bountiful harvest.

I would explore every corner
of this wondrous earth,

and delight in all our differences.

If I were the sun, I would laugh loudly and freely, giving thanks for this gift of life.

Oh, to be the sun! To swing and sway
with the mountains and trees

and dance across luminous waters.

I wish I were the sun
so that I might keep my
friends warm and cozy
on a winter afternoon.

And if I were the sun,
I would rest peacefully
at the end of a busy day...

. . . knowing tomorrow I would shine once more.